For Alek and Kyle.
For REAL.

For Alek and Kyle.
For REAL.

3

Hey, Hog!
Let's pretend to be
Elephant and Piggie!

That sounds
hard, Harold.

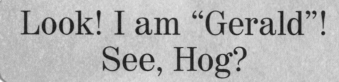

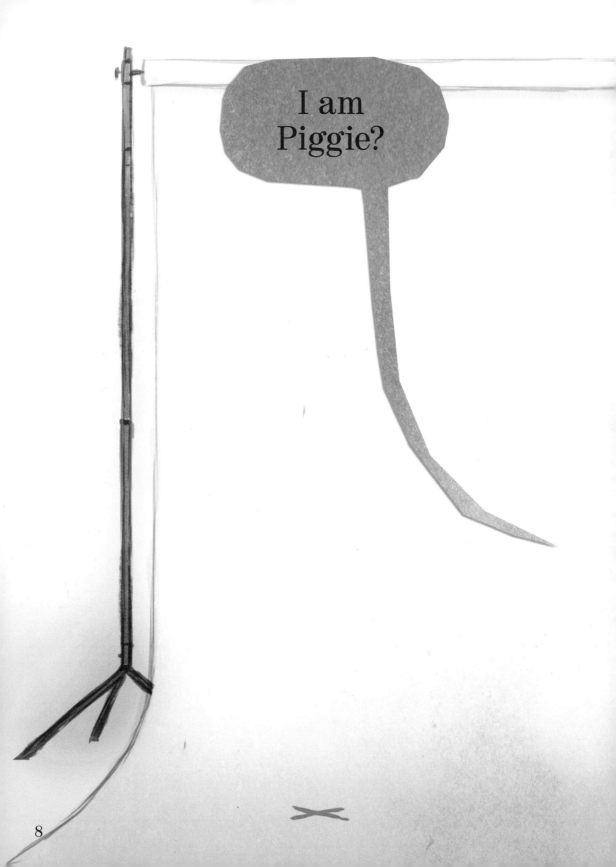

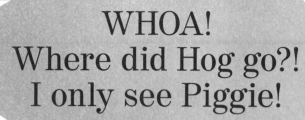

11

ALL AT THE SAME TIME!

STOP!

Gerald would not smile . . .
and dance . . .
and fly . . .

ALL AT THE SAME TIME!

You are so lucky, "Piggie."

You get to *smile* . . .

and *dance* . . .

26

29

30

31

But they are
best friends, like us.

If we cannot pretend
to be best friends—

Then maybe . . .

34

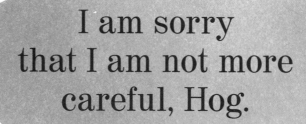

39

43

44

It is fun to *pretend* to be best friends.

When you really *are* best friends.

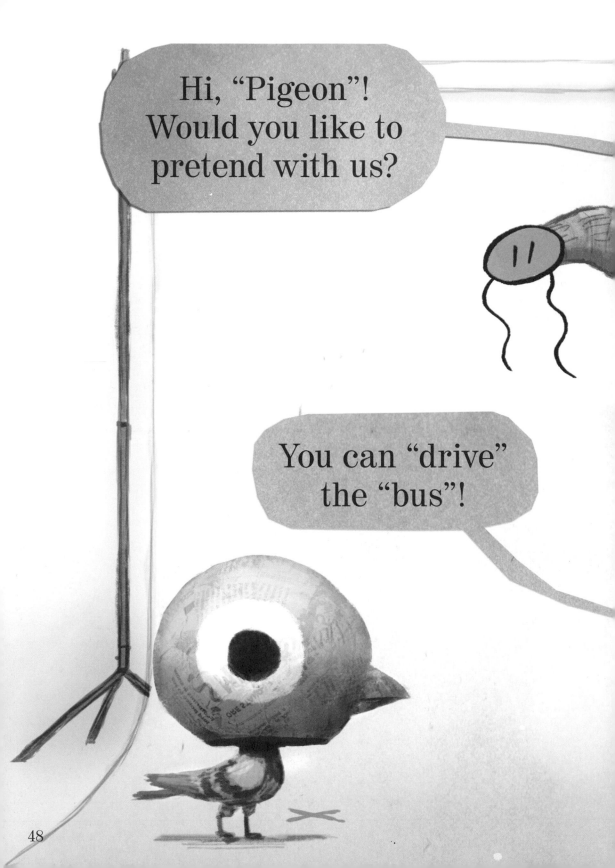

48

LET'S PRETEND TO BE "HAROLD AND HOG"!!!

First Edition, May 2019 • 3 5 7 9 10 8 6 4 2 • FAC-029191-19150 • Printed in Malaysia
This book is set in Century 725/Monotype; Grilled Cheese BTN/Fontbros, with hand-lettering by Dan Santat and Mo Willems

Library of Congress Cataloging-in-Publication Data

Names: Willems, Mo, author, illustrator. • Santat, Dan, author, illustrator. • Title: Harold & Hog pretend for real! by [Mo Willems and] Dan Santat. • Other titles: Harold and Hog pretend for real! Description: First edition. • New York : Hyperion Books for Children, an imprint of Disney Book Group, 2019. Series: Elephant & Piggie Like Reading! ; [6] • Summary: Can the friendship of best friends Harold and Hog, a carefree elephant and a careful hog, survive a game of pretending to be Mo Willems's Elephant and Piggie? Identifiers: LCCN 2018053319 • ISBN 9781368027168 (paper over board) • Subjects: • CYAC: Best friends— Fiction. • Friendship—Fiction. • Imagination—Fiction. • Characters in literature—Fiction. • Humorous stories. • Classification: LCC PZ7.W65535 Hb 2019 • DDC [E]—dc23
LC record available at https://lccn.loc.gov/2018053319

Reinforced binding
Visit hyperionbooksforchildren.com and pigeonpresents.com